W9-BEU-170

Copyright ©1998 by La Galera.
Originally published in Spanish
by La Galera under the title "Cabellos de Oro"
All rights reserved.

Text design by Amy Nathan.
Typeset in Weiss and Handle Old Style.
Printed in Singapore.

Library of Congress Cataloging-in-Publication Data
Mata, Marta.
Goldilocks and the three bears =
Ricitos de oro y los tres osos /
adapted by Marta Mata; illustrations by Arnal Ballester;
translated to Spanish by Alis Alejandro.
p. cm.
Summary: A retelling of the classic story of
Goldilocks and the three bears.
ISBN: 0-8118- 2075-0 (HC) 0-8118-1835-7 (PB)
[1. Folklore. 2. Bears—Folklore. 3. Spanish language
materials—Bilingual.] I. Ballester, Arnal, ill.
II. Goldilocks and the three bears. English. III. Title.
PZ74.1.M35 1998
398.22—dc21
97-28902
CIP
AC

Distributed in Canada by Raincoast Books
8680 Cambie Street, Vancouver, British Columbia V6P 6M9

10 9 8 7 6 5 4 3 2 1

Chronicle Books
85 Second Street, San Francisco, California 94105

Website: www.chronbooks.com

GOLDILOCKS AND THE THREE BEARS

RICITOS DE ORO Y LOS TRES OSOS

ADAPTATION BY MARTA MATA
ILLUSTRATIONS BY ARNAL BALLESTER
SPANISH TRANSLATION BY ALIS ALEJANDRO

chronicle books · san francisco

One day, Goldilocks went for a walk in the forest. In the middle of the forest, she saw a little house.

Un día, Ricitos de Oro paseaba por el bosque y en medio del bosque vio una casita.

The door of the house was open. Goldilocks decided to go inside.

~

Como la puerta de la casa estaba abierta Ricitos de Oro decidió entrar.

Tired from her walk, Goldilocks wanted to rest.
   First, she sat in a big chair: but it was too hard.
   Then, she sat in a medium chair: but is was too soft.
   Finally, she sat in a little chair: and it was just right—until it broke!

Cansada por haber caminado tanto, Ricitos de Oro quiso descansar.
   Primero se sentó en una silla grande: pero era muy dura.
   Luego se sentó en una silla mediana: pero era muy blanda.
   Finalmente se sentó en una silla pequeña: era perfecta, pero se rompió.

Goldilocks stood up and felt very hungry.

First, she ate soup from a big bowl: but it was too hot.

Then, she ate soup from a medium bowl: but it was too cold.

Finally, she ate soup from a little bowl: and it was just right. Goldilocks gobbled it all up.

Ricitos de Oro se paró y sintió mucha hambre.

Primero probó sopa de un plato grande: pero estaba muy caliente.

Luego probó sopa de un plato mediano: pero estaba muy fría.

Finalmente probó sopa de un plato pequeño: estaba perfecta. Ricitos de Oro se tomó toda la sopa rápidamente.

After lunch, Goldilocks was sleepy.
First, she lay down in a big bed: but it was too high.
Then, she lay down in a medium bed: but it was too low.
Finally, she lay down in a little bed: and it was just right.
Goldilocks fell fast asleep.

Después de comer, Ricitos de Oro tuvo sueño.
Primero se acostó en una cama grande: pero era muy dura.
Luego se acostó en una cama mediana: pero era muy blanda.
Finalmente se acostó en una cama pequeña: era perfecta.
Ricitos de Oro se quedó profundamente dormida.

No sooner was Goldilocks asleep, than three bears walked into the house.

～

Apenas Ricitos de Oro se quedó dormida, tres osos entraron a la casa.

"Someone's been sitting in my chair," said Papa Bear.
   "Someone's been sitting in my chair," said Mama Bear.
   "Someone's been sitting in my chair... and they broke it," said Baby Bear.

—

—Alguien se sentó en mi silla —dijo Papá Oso.
   —Alguien se sentó en mi silla —dijo Mamá Osa.
   —Alguien se sentó en mi silla... y la rompió —dijo Osito.

"Someone's been eating my soup," said Papa Bear.
   "Someone's been eating my soup," said Mama Bear.
   "Someone's been eating my soup...and they gobbled it all up," said Baby Bear.

—Alguien probó mi sopa —dijo Papá Oso.
   —Alguien probó mi sopa —dijo Mamá Osa.
   —Alguien probó mi sopa... y se la tomó toda —dijo Osito.

"Someone's been sleeping in my bed," said Papa Bear.
"Someone's been sleeping in my bed," said Mama Bear.
"Someone's been sleeping in my bed...and she is still here!"
said Baby Bear.

—Alguien se acostó en mi cama —dijo Papá Oso.
   —Alguien se acostó en mi cama —dijo Mamá Osa.
   —Alguien se acostó en mi cama... y ahora está durmiendo
en ella —dijo Osito.

Hearing the commotion, Goldilocks woke up. She was so surprised to see the three bears, she jumped out of bed and...

~

Ricitos de Oro se despertó a causa del revuelo y se sorprendió mucho al ver a los tres osos. Ricitos de Oro saltó de la cama y...

...ran through the forest all the way home.

⁓

...cruzó el bosque corriendo hasta llegar a su casa.

Also in this series: **Jack and the Beanstalk**
También en esta serie: **Juan y los frijoles mágicos**